MR. GRUMPY

by Roger Hargreaves

It was a lovely summer evening.

Mr Grumpy was at home.

Crosspatch Cottage!

He sat down in an armchair, and picked up a book.

And then, do you know what he did?

He tore all the pages out of it!

Every one!

Mr Grumpy can't stand books.

He has a shocking bad temper.

In fact, he's quite the most bad-tempered person you can imagine.

Grumpy by name, and even more grumpy by nature!

The following morning, he was out in his garden pulling up flowers (he couldn't stand pretty flowers growing in his garden), when out of the corner of his eye he saw a figure.

It was Mr Happy.

"Good morning," said Mr Happy.

"Good?" said Mr Grumpy. "What's good about it?"

"But . . .," said Mr Happy.

"But nothing," went on Mr Grumpy. "Get out of my garden!"

"I beg your pardon?" said Mr Happy.

"You heard me," snapped Mr Grumpy. "Go away!"

"I say," laughed Mr Happy. "You are a bad-tempered fellow!"

"Hmph!" grunted Mr Grumpy.

"And," went on Mr Happy, "bad-tempered fellows need to change their ways."

"Rubbish!" retorted Mr Grumpy and went into his cottage, deliberately stepping on Mr Happy's foot as he passed him.

"Ouch!" said Mr Happy.

BANG! went the door of Crosspatch Cottage as Mr Grumpy slammed it behind him.

Mr Happy stood there, looking not quite so happy as he normally does.

His foot hurt!

He thought.

And thought.

And thought some more.

Then, he had an idea.

He smiled, and went to see Mr Tickle.

Mr Happy told Mr Tickle of his idea of how to get Mr Grumpy to change his ways, and Mr Tickle grinned the sort of grin that goes from ear to ear.

That is, if you have ears, which he doesn't.

"Oh," he grinned, rubbing the hands at the end of those extraordinarily long arms of his together. "That sounds fun!"

That afternoon, Mr Grumpy went to town, shopping.

He walked into Mr Meat's shop.

Mr Meat was a butcher.

"Give me some sausages," snapped Mr Grumpy. "And be quick about it!"

Poor Mr Meat, who was frightened of Mr Grumpy, did as he was told.

But, as he was doing as he was told, something appeared through his shop doorway.

Do you know what it was?

It was an extraordinarily long arm belonging to . . .

Well, you can guess who it belonged to.

Can't you?

That extraordinarily long arm of Mr Tickle's came in through the door, and across the shop, and up to Mr Grumpy, and tickled him.

"Oh!" squeaked Mr Grumpy in alarm, dropping his sausages, and looking round to see what had happened.

But, could he see anything?

He could not!

"Hmph!" grunted Mr Grumpy, and picked up his sausages, and went next door.

To the cake shop.

CRASH! went the door of the shop.

"Give me a cake," snapped Mr Grumpy. "And hurry up!"

Poor Mrs Fairy, who sold cakes, was frightened of Mr Grumpy, so did as she was told.

But, as she was doing as she was told, guess what happened?

"Oh!" squeaked Mr Grumpy, dropping his cake, and his sausages.

He just could not understand what was happening.

And, the same thing happened at Mr Daily's (the newspaper shop), and at Mrs Humbug's (the sweetshop), and at Mr Bottle's dairy, and at Mr Packet's (the grocer's).

It went on all afternoon!

And all afternoon Mr Grumpy kept being tickled, and dropping his shopping, and picking it up, and being tickled, and dropping his shopping, and picking it up, and being tickled, and dropping his shopping, and . . .

He just could not understand it.

On his way home to Crosspatch Cottage, he met Mr Happy again.

"Hello," grinned Mr Happy. "Having a nice day?"

"Get out of my way," snapped Mr Grumpy, "before I kick you!"

But, almost before the words had passed his lips, that extraordinarily long arm of Mr Tickle's had appeared from behind a tree and tickled him yet again.

He jumped in the air, and dropped all his shopping (yet again), and fell over.

Mr Happy looked down at Mr Grumpy lying amid a jumble of sausages and cake and newspapers and sweets and milk and cornflakes.

"I think," he laughed, "that if you were to change your ways and be not quite so bad-tempered quite so often, this sort of thing might not happen to you quite so often."

"Hmph!" grunted Mr Grumpy.

He picked up all his shopping (yet again) and went home to Crosspatch Cottage.

But on his way he did think about what Mr Happy had said, because he very definitely did not like what had happened to him that afternoon.

Mr Happy and Mr Tickle laughed and shook hands.

And so, after that, he did try to be not quite so bad-tempered quite so often.

And, the more he tried the less he found he was tickled, and so he tried more and more, and these days he's quite a changed person.

Why, only the other evening, he picked up a book, and do you know what?

He only tore out one page!

3 Great Offers for MR. MEN Fans!

MR. MEN TOKEN

1 New Mr. Men or Little Miss Library Bus Presentation Cases

A brand new stronger, roomier school bus library box, with sturdy carrying handle and stay-closed fasteners.

The full colour, wipe-clean boxes make a great home for your full collection.

They're just £5.99 inc P&P and free bookmark!

☐ MR. MEN   ☐ LITTLE MISS (please tick and order overleaf)

2 Door Hangers and Posters

In every Mr. Men and Little Miss book like this one, you will find a special token. Collect 6 tokens and we will send you a brilliant Mr. Men or Little Miss poster and a Mr. Men or Little Miss double sided full colour bedroom door hanger of your choice. Simply tick your choice in the list and tape a 50p coin for your two items to this page.

PLEASE STICK YOUR 50P COIN HERE

Door Hangers (please tick)
☐ Mr. Nosey & Mr. Muddle
☐ Mr. Slow & Mr. Busy
☐ Mr. Messy & Mr. Quiet
☐ Mr. Perfect & Mr. Forgetful
☐ Little Miss Fun & Little Miss Late
☐ Little Miss Helpful & Little Miss Tidy
☐ Little Miss Busy & Little Miss Brainy
☐ Little Miss Star & Little Miss Fun

Posters (please tick)
☐ MR. MEN
☐ LITTLE MISS

3 Sixteen Beautiful Fridge Magnets – any 2 for £2.00! inc.P&P

They're very special collector's items!
Simply tick your first and second* choices from the list below
of any 2 characters!

1st Choice

- ☐ Mr. Happy
- ☐ Mr. Lazy
- ☐ Mr. Topsy-Turvy
- ☐ Mr. Bounce
- ☐ Mr. Bump
- ☐ Mr. Small
- ☐ Mr. Snow
- ☐ Mr. Wrong

- ☐ Mr. Daydream
- ☐ Mr. Tickle
- ☐ Mr. Greedy
- ☐ Mr. Funny
- ☐ Little Miss Giggles
- ☐ Little Miss Splendid
- ☐ Little Miss Naughty
- ☐ Little Miss Sunshine

2nd Choice

- ☐ Mr. Happy
- ☐ Mr. Lazy
- ☐ Mr. Topsy-Turvy
- ☐ Mr. Bounce
- ☐ Mr. Bump
- ☐ Mr. Small
- ☐ Mr. Snow
- ☐ Mr. Wrong

- ☐ Mr. Daydream
- ☐ Mr. Tickle
- ☐ Mr. Greedy
- ☐ Mr. Funny
- ☐ Little Miss Giggles
- ☐ Little Miss Splendid
- ☐ Little Miss Naughty
- ☐ Little Miss Sunshine

*Only in case your first choice is out of stock.

--- **TO BE COMPLETED BY AN ADULT** ---

**To apply for any of these great offers, ask an adult to complete the coupon below and send it with
the appropriate payment and tokens, if needed, to MR. MEN OFFERS, PO BOX 7, MANCHESTER M19 2HD**

- ☐ Please send _____ Mr. Men Library case(s) and/or _____ Little Miss Library case(s) at £5.99 each inc P&P
- ☐ Please send a poster and door hanger as selected overleaf. I enclose six tokens plus a 50p coin for P&P
- ☐ Please send me _____ pair(s) of Mr. Men/Little Miss fridge magnets, as selected above at £2.00 inc P&P

Fan's Name _____

Address _____

_____ **Postcode** _____

Date of Birth _____

Name of Parent/Guardian _____

Total amount enclosed £ _____

- ☐ **I enclose a cheque/postal order payable to Egmont Books Limited**
- ☐ **Please charge my MasterCard/Visa/Amex/Switch or Delta account** (delete as appropriate)

Card Number

Expiry date ___/___ **Signature** _____

Please allow 28 days for delivery. Offer is only available while stocks last. We reserve the right to change the terms
of this offer at any time and we offer a 14 day money back guarantee. This does not affect your statutory rights.
Data Protection Act: If you do not wish to receive other similar offers from us or companies we recommend, please
tick this box ☐. Offers apply to UK only.

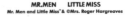

MR.MEN   LITTLE MISS
Mr. Men and Little Miss™ & ©Mrs. Roger Hargreaves

CUT ALONG DOTTED LINE AND RETURN THIS WHOLE PAGE